This Little Tiger book belongs to:

_____

_____

_____

For Jake J A, with love ~ M C B

For Kerry James ~ T M

LITTLE TIGER PRESS
An imprint of Magi Publications
1 The Coda Centre, 189 Munster Road, London SW6 6AW
www.littletigerpress.com

First published in Great Britain 2011
This edition published 2011
Text copyright © M Christina Butler 2011
Illustrations copyright © Tina Macnaughton 2011
M Christina Butler and Tina Macnaughton have asserted their
rights to be identified as the author and illustrator of this work
under the Copyright, Designs and Patents Act, 1988

A CIP catalogue record for this book is available from the
British Library

Printed in China • LTP/1800/0214/0411

10 9 8 7 6 5 4 3 2 1

One Christmas Night

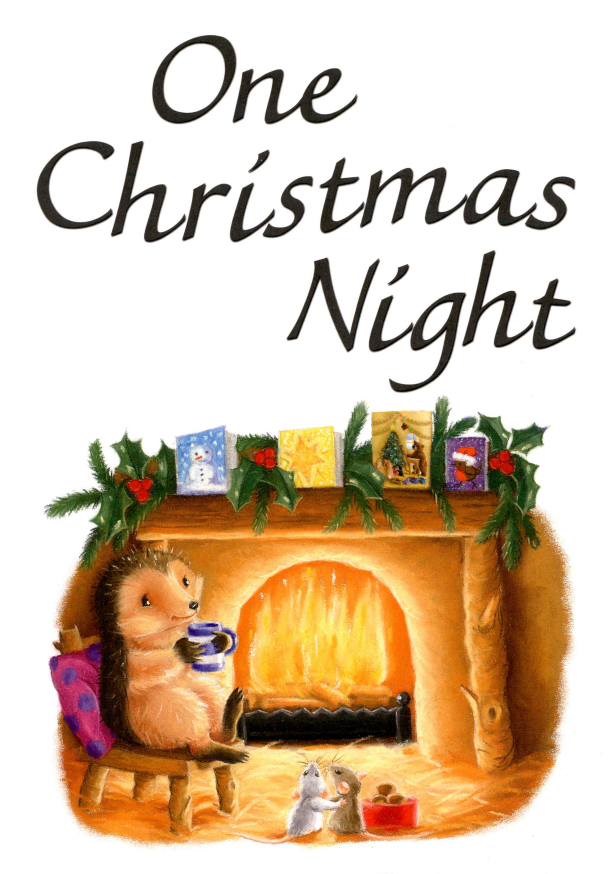

M Christina Butler   Illustrated by Tina Macnaughton

LITTLE TIGER PRESS
London

It was nearly Christmas and
Little Hedgehog just could not wait.
"Mince pies and Christmas
cake – yum yum!" he laughed.
"Ooh, now I can put up the big shiny
star that Badger gave me."

"Perfect!" cried Little Hedgehog as he fixed the star to the very top of his tree.

Then he opened Badger's card. "How lovely," he said. It had a huge, glittering Christmas tree on the front.

"Oh dear! My house isn't Christmassy and my tree doesn't sparkle like that," he sighed.

Just then a *rat-a-tat-tat!* came at the door.

"Happy Christmas!" cried Mouse.

"Thank you," said Little Hedgehog.
"But Mouse, I don't know what to do!
My house just isn't Christmassy at all."
"We'll soon fix that," Mouse smiled.

"We can make pine cones sparkle with glitter," said Mouse as they tramped into the woods.

"Take cover!" cried Little Hedgehog as the cones came tumbling down.

"There's holly for the fireplace," Mouse said.

"Ouch!" squeaked Little Hedgehog. "It has more prickles than me!"

"Chestnuts and acorns, and big bowls of berries!" they all sang as they marched home.

Together they glued and glittered until nuts
and acorns twinkled like stars, and holly twigs
shimmered red, green and gold.

"Wow!" cried Little Hedgehog.
"It's like a magic Christmassy cave!" said Mouse. "But we have to go. We haven't wrapped our presents yet."

"Oh no!" squeaked Little Hedgehog. "Presents? I've forgotten to get presents for my friends!"

Little Hedgehog thought hard. "I know – I can give this book to Badger!"

"I'll make a carrot cake for Rabbit."

"And a night-time picture for Fox."

"I can make stockings full of nuts for the little ones," chuckled Little Hedgehog, pattering into the wood again.

He gazed up at the glittering branches as snowflakes floated past his nose. "And a big bunch of twinkly twigs for Mouse," he smiled.

Little Hedgehog wandered on and on
through the trees, looking for the best
twigs he could find. The wood grew
darker and the snowflakes swirled faster
around him.

"Phew!" he gasped, struggling
with the basket. "However
shall I get home?"

At last the snow stopped, and a bright moon peeped above the trees. Pale blue shadows flitted here and there as Little Hedgehog huffed and puffed through the snow. Then, in the stillness, he heard a *pad-pad-padding* noise getting closer and closer, until . . .

...*CRASH!*

"Eeek!" yelped Fox,
bumping into Little
Hedgehog.

"You look like a walking
Christmas tree!"

Little Hedgehog and Fox
chuckled and chatted all
the way back home.

Fox put the presents round the tree. "Everything looks lovely!" he said.

But Little Hedgehog was not sure. "There is *still* something missing."

Suddenly, a loud knock came at the door . . .

. . . and in walked Badger, with Rabbit and the mice.
   "Of course!" squeaked Little Hedgehog, clapping
his paws. "That's what was missing – all of my friends!
Happy Christmas, everyone!"

Give the perfect present
with these Little Tiger books!

One Winter's Day

M Christina Butler
Illustrated by Tina Macnaughton

Oh Dylan!

Tracey Corderoy   Tina Macnaughton

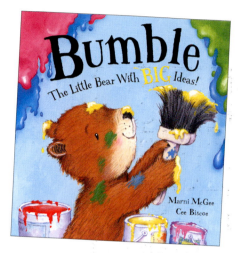

Bumble
The Little Bear With BIG Ideas!

Marni McGee
Cee Biscoe

Rhino's Great BIG Itch!

Natalie Chivers

Snow Friends

M Christina Butler and Tina Macnaughton

One Special Day

M Christina Butler   Tina Macnaughton

For information regarding any of the above titles
or for our catalogue, please contact us:
Little Tiger Press, 1 The Coda Centre,
189 Munster Road, London SW6 6AW
Tel: 020 7385 6333
Fax: 020 7385 7333
E-mail: info@littletiger.co.uk
www.littletigerpress.com